THE CURIOUS SCIENCE QUEST

ROCKY ROAD TO GALILEO

WHAT IS OUR PLACE IN THE SOLAR SYSTEM?

JULIA GOLDING

WITH ANDREW BRIGGS AND ROGER WAGNER

ILLUSTRATIONS BRETT HUDSON

LION CHILDREN'S

Published by Lion Children's Books
an imprint of
Lion Hudson Limited
Wilkinson House, Jordan Hill Business Park,
Banbury Road, Oxford OX2 8DR, England
www.lionhudson.com/lionchildrens

ISBN 978 0 7459 7752 2
e-ISBN 978 0 7459 7759 1

First edition 2018

Acknowledgments
This publication was made possible through the support of a grant from Templeton Religion Trust. The opinions expressed in this publication are those of the authors and do not necessarily reflect the views of Templeton Religion Trust.

A catalogue record for this book is available from the British Library
Printed and bound in the UK, September 2018, LH26

THE CURIOUS SCIENCE QUEST

"The brilliant and entertaining illustrations in this series enliven a clear and enjoyable text that should stimulate serious thought about the world and our place in it."

LORD REES
Astronomer Royal, President of the Royal Society 2005–2010

"Too often science and faith are pitted against each other. This book breaks down that split in a creative and engaging way. It shows the scope of science in our lives and how the study of science and the study of God feed and magnify each other. Human beings have always been hungry for understanding and meaning, and this book beautifully shows how this has worked out from the earliest time. It is a book that leaves me in awe at the 'art' of science: for the way it unveils the magnificence of God our Creator, who stretches out the canvas."

MOST REVEREND JUSTIN WELBY
Archbishop of Canterbury

"A witty and accessible treasure trove of scientific discoveries that goes to the heart of our human quest to understand who we are. This book doesn't dumb down or gloss over imponderables but will leave you marvelling at the science and asking for more."

PROFESSOR REBECCA FITZGERALD
Director of Medical Studies, University of Cambridge
Lister Prize Fellowship (2008), NHS Innovation (2011), NIHR Research Professorship (2013)

"Has the bug bitten you? Are you curious? Curious to know how the universe evolved from the Big Bang? How matter arranges itself into objects ranging from atomic nuclei to human beings, planets, and stars? Are you curious to know why all these things are the way they are?

Science is good for the 'how' questions but does not necessarily have the answers on the 'why' questions. Can science and religion talk to each other? Enjoy this series and learn more about science and the enriching dialogue between science and faith."

PROFESSOR ROLF HEUER
Director General of CERN from 2009 to 2015
President of the German Physical Society and President of the SESAME Council

"Here is a wonderful and wittily written introduction to science as the art of asking open questions and not jumping to conclusions. It's also an amusing excursion through evolution and anthropology which packs in a lot of learning with the lightest of touches. A much-needed antidote to the bludgeoning crudity of so much writing in both science and religion."

REVEREND DOCTOR MALCOLM GUITE
Poet, singer-songwriter, priest, and academic
Chaplain at Girton College Cambridge

CONTENTS

INTRODUCTION

Life is full of big questions, what we might call ultimate questions. In the first two parts of the Curious Quest our intrepid time travellers, Harriet and Milton, explored two of the most important mysteries:

- When did humans start to ask questions?
- Who were the first scientists?

They discovered that investigating our place in the world goes back far beyond recorded history. They then visited the people of Ancient Greece who started asking big picture questions, such as "what came first?". The Greeks also asked more detailed ones about how things work – and thus invented science!

Then disaster struck our time travellers. They were about to set out on the next stage in their mission when Harriet was tortoise-napped by an Alexandrian scientist called Simplicius. Milton is now on a desperate quest to rescue her.

Our Time Travelling Guides

Meet our guides to the ultimate questions.

Harriet is a tortoise. She was collected by Charles Darwin on his famous voyage on *The Beagle* (1831–36), which was when he explored the world and saw many things that led him to the Theory of Evolution. Harriet was brought back in his suitcase to England to be the family pet. As a tortoise she can live for a very long time and is well over a hundred.

Milton is a cat. He belongs to the famous twentieth-century physicist, Erwin Schrödinger, and inspired some of his owner's best ideas. Milton is not very good at making up his mind.

Curious Quest

Having noticed some curious words over the entrance to a famous laboratory in Cambridge University, Harriet and Milton decided to go on a quest to find out the answers to as many ultimate questions as they could. In fact, they agreed to travel in time to see all the important events in the history of science.

In this series, you are invited to go with them. But look out for the Curiosity Bug hidden in some intriguing places. See how many of these you can count. Answer on page 110.

But first, of course, Milton has to rescue Harriet. Where on earth has she ended up?

HARRIET

Milton Flies to the Rescue: The Islamic Golden Age

As the time machine spins through space and time, Milton is desperately trying to understand the controls. Until now, he has always relied on Harriet to do the driving so is feeling very out of his depth.

"I'm sure there is a tracking device somewhere. Harriet is too clever not to have thought of that," says Milton. He finds a dial hidden under a scroll they picked up in Athens. A little screen marked "Harriet" is flashing.

His fur stands up on end. "What kind of danger?" squeaks Milton.

The message changes.

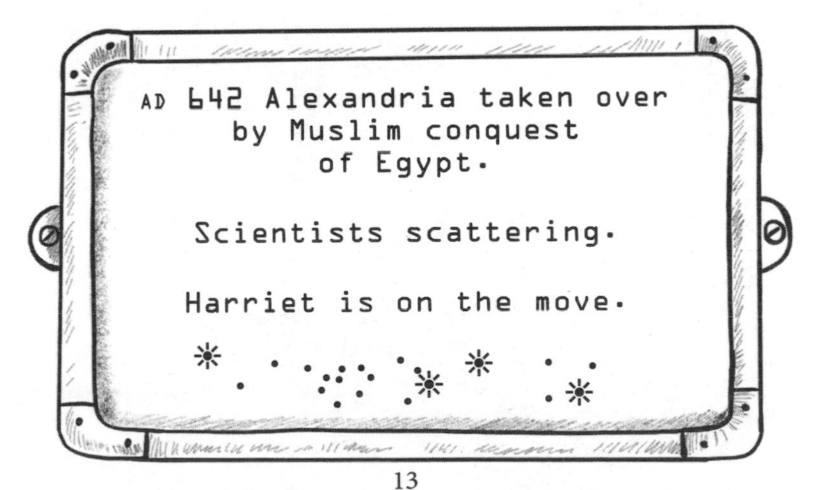

"Oh no, Harriet is in the middle of all that! Time Machine, where and when do we have our best chance to rescue Harriet?"

There is a whirring deep in the workings of the machine and then a light blips on the screen.

"Harriet is in Baghdad in – what's this? AD 830?" Milton knows that tortoises can live for a very long time but he is worried that even Harriet might not survive centuries. "Is she all right?"

I'm protecting her,

writes the time machine.

While you are both travelling in the past before your real birthday I can keep you out of time.

"How?"

As time can't be certain where you are – then, now, here, there – it can't age you.

Milton mews a sigh of relief. "Another time paradox! Handy."

I thought so,

writes the time machine, rather smugly in Milton's view.

Your best opportunity to save her is when she arrives at the House of Wisdom. This is also your next stop on the Curious Science Quest.

"Take me there, please." Even if the machine does sound too pleased with itself, Milton is rather relieved that it has started talking to him. He wasn't certain he'd end up anywhere near where he needed to be if *his* paws were on the controls. He has yet to pass his Time Travel Machine driving test.

The machine begins to hum a new harmonic note as it changes course. It sounds to Milton as if the machine does know what it is doing so he begins to relax.

"While we're travelling, Time Machine, can you show me what is happening out in the world so I know what I'm facing?"

The machine's answer is to print out a timeline that Milton suspects Harriet has prepared for him.

Harriet's Guide to the Golden Age of Islamic Science

- 642 Greek Christian culture of Alexandria swept away in Muslim conquest of Egypt
- c.690 Arabic now the common language of the Middle East
- 762 Abbasid Caliph (ruler) Al-Mansur founds Baghdad
- c.780 Birth of Muhammad ibn Musa al-Khwarizmi, later a scholar in the House of Wisdom, who invented algebra and introduced Indian numerals
- c.801 Birth of Al-Kindi, later known as Philosopher of the Arabs
- c.810 House of Wisdom set up in Baghdad under Abbasid Caliphs Al-Mansur and his son, Al-Ma'mun, making the city the new centre of scientific thought
- c.1020 Avicenna's *Canon of Medicine*, influential on medicine for many centuries
- 1021 Ibn al-Haytham's *Book of Optics*, sometimes said to be the first book of experimental science
- 1085 Fall of Toledo, bringing Islamic scholarship and Greek scientific writings to Christian world
- 1126 Birth of Ibn Rusd (Averroes) in Cordoba, known for his work on force and kinetic energy, also popularized Aristotle in Christian Europe through his commentaries

House of Wisdom, Baghdad

The time machine lands in front of a grand white building.[1]

Welcome to the greatest collection of books in the world today! flashes up on the screen. *Printed on the newest invention: paper – a technology all the way from China!*

"The library at Alexandria has gone, so Baghdad has taken over," says Milton. "They've replaced old papyrus technology with this new import from the Far East. Thank you, Time Machine."

Milton hesitates at the door. He isn't used to going out on his own without Harriet. "Come on, stop being such a scaredy cat: she needs you!" he tells himself. Putting his best paw forward, he ventures outside.

A busy city greets him. Roads enter through four huge gates, one at each point of the compass. People are coming and going, bringing goods from all over the known world. From the kicks aimed in his direction when he doesn't move fast enough, Milton realizes no one worships cats anymore, not like they did in Alexandria. He feels quite overwhelmed by the hubbub but he is getting close to Harriet – he can sense it with his whiskers.

Entering an elegant building of high ceilings and courtyards, Milton finds himself in the heart of the House of Wisdom. He pokes his head cautiously in one room and sees turban-wearing scholars seated on cushions, debating how best to measure time and how to find the direction of prayer towards Mecca.

1 As archaeologists are yet to find trace of the House of Wisdom, some experts say it didn't exist as a single place, but was a collection of scholars in different households. However, Milton says: "Absence of evidence isn't evidence of absence!"

Milton listens to their debate for a few minutes. "Harriet would be interested in that," Milton mutters. "In their big picture of the world, these Islamic thinkers have decided God wants them to find out about his world. And they have a real use for scientific knowledge as it helps them be better at their prayers."

But there is no sign of a tortoise. Moving on, he sneaks into another chamber and finds translators busy working on recognizable scrolls of Greek science. He hears one mention Aristotle so takes this as a good sign he is on familiar ground. Cautiously, Milton approaches.

"Excuse me, sir?"

The man looks down at him, his splendid black beard and moustache better groomed than Milton's fur. "Peace be with you, little cat. I am Muhammad ibn Musa al-Khwarizmi." He bows. "May I help you?"

Milton jumps up on to the desk where the man has his papers spread out. "I'm looking for a tortoise called Harriet. Have you seen her?"

The man scratches Milton's chin. "I can't say that I have. Where did you last see her?"

"About 280 years ago, or fifteen minutes, depending on how you look at these things."

"Good gracious, what an interesting pair of numbers!" The scholar quite forgets he is supposed to be helping Milton and begins to chalk figures out on a blackboard. "In the old days we would have written that like this."

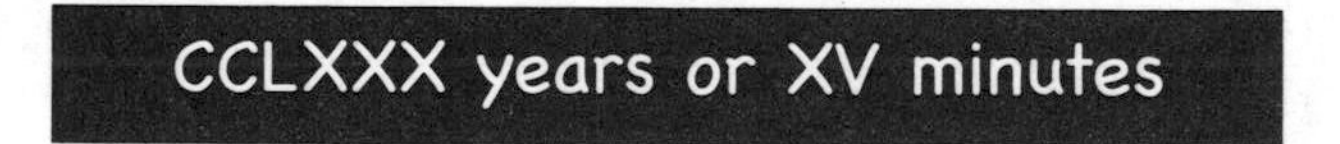

"But now I can write it this way, using the number system of India."

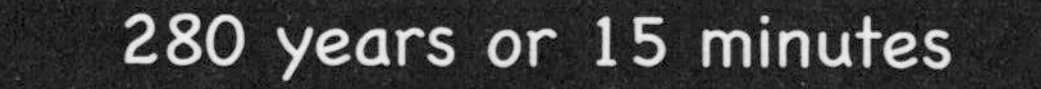

"See how superior the new way is? Look at clever zero. It can show you how many tens, hundreds, and so on there are in a number. We can get rid of all those confusing letters."

(Mostly) Wrong Ideas: The Curious Case of Zero

One of the common mostly wrong ideas is that we got our number zero from Arabic mathematicians. In fact there are at least three possible sources for the idea that pre-date these clever scholars by some way:

1) Enter the early birds. Some 2,000 years earlier, the Babylonians used a placeholder in counting – the function that 0 performs in numbers like 2000, telling us the 2 is there to count units of a thousand. (Amazingly, the Mayans in Central America were also doing something similar in their calendar, independent of the West.)

2) Zero as nothing. Harriet and Milton's old friend from Ancient Athens, the philosopher Aristotle, is one of those often given credit for being the first to talk about the concept of nothingness or, in his terms, vacuum.

3) Indian mathematicians in around AD 450 started using zero as part of their number system – and this is the most likely source for the idea in Arabic maths.

"That's very good, but I still want to find Harriet. We were with John Philoponus and Simplicius…"

"Ah! The scholars from Alexandria - then that's where you must look. I'll ask my Christian friend, Hunan ibn Ishaq, to help. He is the world's best finder of things."

MEET THE SCIENTIST

MUHAMMAD IBN MUSA AL-KHWARIZMI

- Lived: 780–850 AD
- Number of Jobs: 3 (mathematician, geographer and astronomer)
- Influence (out of 100): 90, introduces our number system from India
- Right? (out of 20): 19, introduces important concepts in mathematics and, thanks to him, many maths words come from Arabic, like algebra
- Helpfully Wrong? (out of 10): 0, he seems to get most things right!
- Interesting Fact (out of 10): 7, the mathematical term "algorithm", the process used by computer programs, comes from the Latin version of his name – Algoritmi

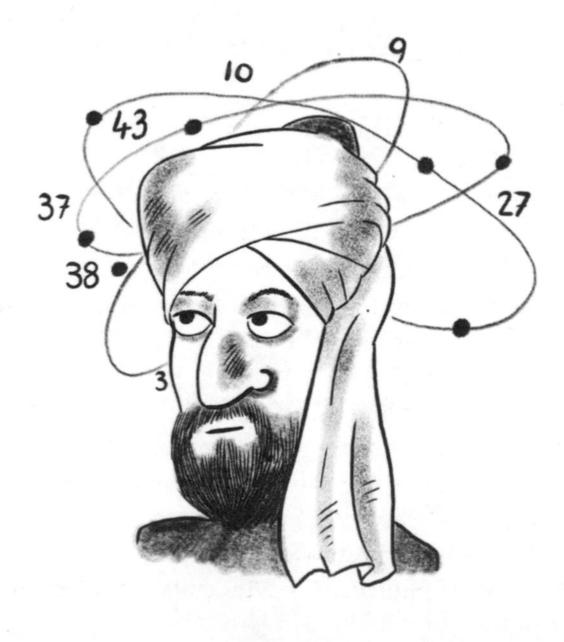

Milton and Muhammad find Hunan ibn Ishaq working on a translation.

"How were your travels, Hunan?" asks Muhammad.

"Excellent! I think I've found another scroll by the Roman doctor Galen. My medical handbook is almost complete."

Milton isn't interested in traveller's tales; he is anxious about Harriet. "Do we have to talk about musty old books? I'm on a tortoise rescue mission!"

Both scholars look at him in amazement.

"But if we don't translate these works from Greek, then so much knowledge will be lost to the world. If the new owners can't read them, they won't know how valuable they are and they will throw them out. I tell you, little cat, what people do with old scrolls is shocking!" exclaims Hunan. "It's a race against time to save as many as I can."

MILTON'S NOTEPAD: USES FOR OLD SCROLLS

- Destroyed along with the library holding them (fate of many of those in Alexandria).
- Used as firelighters.
- Ancient recycling – text scraped off and written over.
- Left in a cave (like the famous Dead Sea Scrolls) and forgotten.
- Put on the rubbish heap (sometimes to be found by archaeologists).
- Stored badly so they crumble to dust.
- Stolen and end up in someone else's library...

Milton's whiskers are twitching. "I don't suppose you happened upon a tortoise among the records? About so big?" He holds out his paws to Harriet's approximate size. "Last seen in Alexandria."

"Let me have a look. I'm just unpacking a crate rescued from the library there."

Together Muhammad and Hunan unroll scroll after scroll. Milton notices works by his old friends Plato and Aristotle as well as lots on medicine and astronomy.

"Ah, here is one by a man called Simplicius. I've come across his writings before. He was a firm supporter of everything Aristotle ever wrote," says Hunan.

"That's the fellow!" exclaims Milton. "He tortoise-napped Harriet!"

"Hmm, it does feel heavier than I would expect."

Carefully, the two scholars unroll the large scroll. There in the middle they find a sleeping tortoise.

"Harriet!" Milton tries to shake her awake but nothing happens. "She's not dead, is she?" he asks fearfully.

Hunan gently lifts Harriet and examines her by the window. "No, I think she is in deep hibernation. You have to give her time to wake up."

TRY THIS AT HOME:

While Harriet is waking up, why not try this game with Roman numerals? Work out which first name would score the highest using Roman letters. The system is as follows:

I – I	C – 100
V – 5	D – 500
X – 10	M – 1000
L – 50	

Letters that don't have a number equivalent score zero, and you can use each letter as many times as you like. The only other rule is that it has to be a real name.

Here's an example. Harriet doesn't score much:

0 + 0 + 0 + 0 + 1 + 0 + 0 = 1

If you are Milton, then you do very well:

1000 + 1 + 50 + 0 + 0 + 0 = 1051

Can you think of a name that does better than that?

Can you think of a name that uses the maximum number of different Latin numbers? What does it score?

NB "Mummy" doesn't count as it isn't a proper name – but it would score... well, work it out!

SAVVY SASSANIANS!

The cultural practice of collecting a library survived in part thanks to a civilization that flourished for four hundred years (AD 226–663) in the Middle East. It's one that you may never have heard about before.

Say a big "Hello!" to the Savvy Sassanians.

This empire ruled Persia (modern Iran) and had an official religion called Zoroastrianism. The Sassanians took over parts of the Middle East as the Roman Empire broke up, continuing until challenged by the first rulers of the new Islamic faith.

Zoroastrians – the faith that loves libraries! (Nothing to do with Zorro!)

In their big picture of the universe, they believed that Zoroaster was the source of all truth, religious and scientific. Many of their sacred texts had been destroyed by Alexander the Great's conquests, so they saw it as their duty to collect all the information they could lay their hands on, gathering it together in storehouses, or their own houses of wisdom. Caliph Al-Mansur, who set up Baghdad's famous House of Wisdom, was following in their footsteps.

Harriet begins to stir. She blinks and opens her eyes. "What time is it?"

"About noon," says Hunan, checking the sundial in the courtyard.

"About AD 830," says Milton. "My two new friends helped me find you."

"What happened to me?" asks Harriet.

"It's a long story," says Milton.

"We will leave you to catch up," says Muhammad. "So pleased you found her."

The two scholars hurry back to their important work.

Harriet looks around her. "Last thing I remember is Alexandria. Milton, where are we?"

"We're in Baghdad in the next stop on our Curiosity Quest. In fact, we are in the middle of the Islamic Scientific Golden Age. Have some lettuce."

Harriet tests each of her limbs. "I'm so pleased I didn't sleep through all that. It was vital for advancing learning, as when the Greek and Roman empires crumbled their knowledge was nearly forgotten. What have you learned so far?"

Milton is happy just to sit by his friend as she chews thoughtfully on her leaf. "That the Islamic scholars like maths and they are very good at translating old works into Arabic so they don't get lost."

Harriet nods. "There were many wonderful thinkers – we won't have time to visit them all. But it is awfully interesting, isn't it? It tells us something about the new faith of Islam at this time."

"What does it tell us?"

"That their faith gives their science a push, and their science helps their faith. We are seeing a good example of the slipstream effect when religion and science work well together." She sips a little water. "Ah – that's better! Did your friends tell you about the Caliph's dream?"

Milton's ears twitch. "No. What dream?"

She pushes over a picture from among the papers lying on Hunan's desk. "Here, look at this."

O Caliph, know that wisdom has no race or nationality.
Aristotle's work
To block ideas is to block the kingdom of God.
Fetch me all the works of all the cleverest men there have ever been. We must learn from them!

"So Aristotle came back in a dream?" muses Milton.

"The Caliph was certainly thinking about him when he went to sleep. When he woke, he made sure that his scholars worked out how to be good Muslims *and* good thinkers. The chief one who did that is also to be found around here somewhere. His name is Abu Yusus Ya'qub al-Kindi. I think that's him over there." Harriet points to a scholar hidden by a huge pile of paper. "He wrote three hundred books and is called the 'Philosopher of the Arabs'. But most importantly he said scholars should not be ashamed to admire the truth, or to acquire it, from wherever it comes."

Milton is pleased to find Harriet is back to her old self. "So shall we go and talk to him?"

"Oh no. He's got his hands full arguing about Aristotle's universe with his colleague al-Farabi. Like John Philoponus and Simplicius, they are arguing about whether or not the universe is eternal."

Milton and Harriet head back to the time machine.

"Where next?" asks Milton.

"Thank you for rescuing me, but I think I need a holiday. Let's go to Spain."

"Hang on! If we are curious about Islamic science, why are we going *there*?"

Harriet gives him one of her looks. "Oh, Milton. I think you'd better brush up on your history while we travel."

"Yes!" thinks Milton, "Harriet is definitely back to being her old self."

BUKHARA AND THE SAMANID EMPIRE: RIVALS TO BAGHDAD'S HOUSE OF WISDOM

The Islamic Golden Age did not only take place in Baghdad but flourished wherever scholars were encouraged to think to help their faith journey. One of the most important places was Bukhara (in present day Uzbekistan, central Asia) and their most famous thinker was a man known in the West as Avicenna.

MEET THE SCIENTIST

IBN SINA (AVICENNA)

- Lived: 980–1037 AD
- Number of Jobs: 6, at least (philosopher, astronomer, medic, chemist, geographer, poet...)
- Influence (out of 100): 80, his *Canon of Medicine* was used as THE medical textbook until 1650
- Right (out of 20): 10, a mixed bag – questioned some Aristotelian ideas but edged towards considering the universe eternal
- Helpfully Wrong? (out of 10): 5, good idea to gather medical knowledge but passed on idea of humours which led to wrong treatments
- Interesting Fact (out of 10): 8, became a fully qualified doctor at 18!

Off to Moorish Spain

The time machine lets out a trill of tings and beeps to celebrate Harriet's return.

"Oh, it talks to us now," says Milton.

"What do you mean 'now'? It always has – or will have – oh, time travel is so hard on language!" Harriet ambles over to the control desk and nudges a few dials and switches. "Machine, please can you print out the map of the Islamic world in AD 1100?"

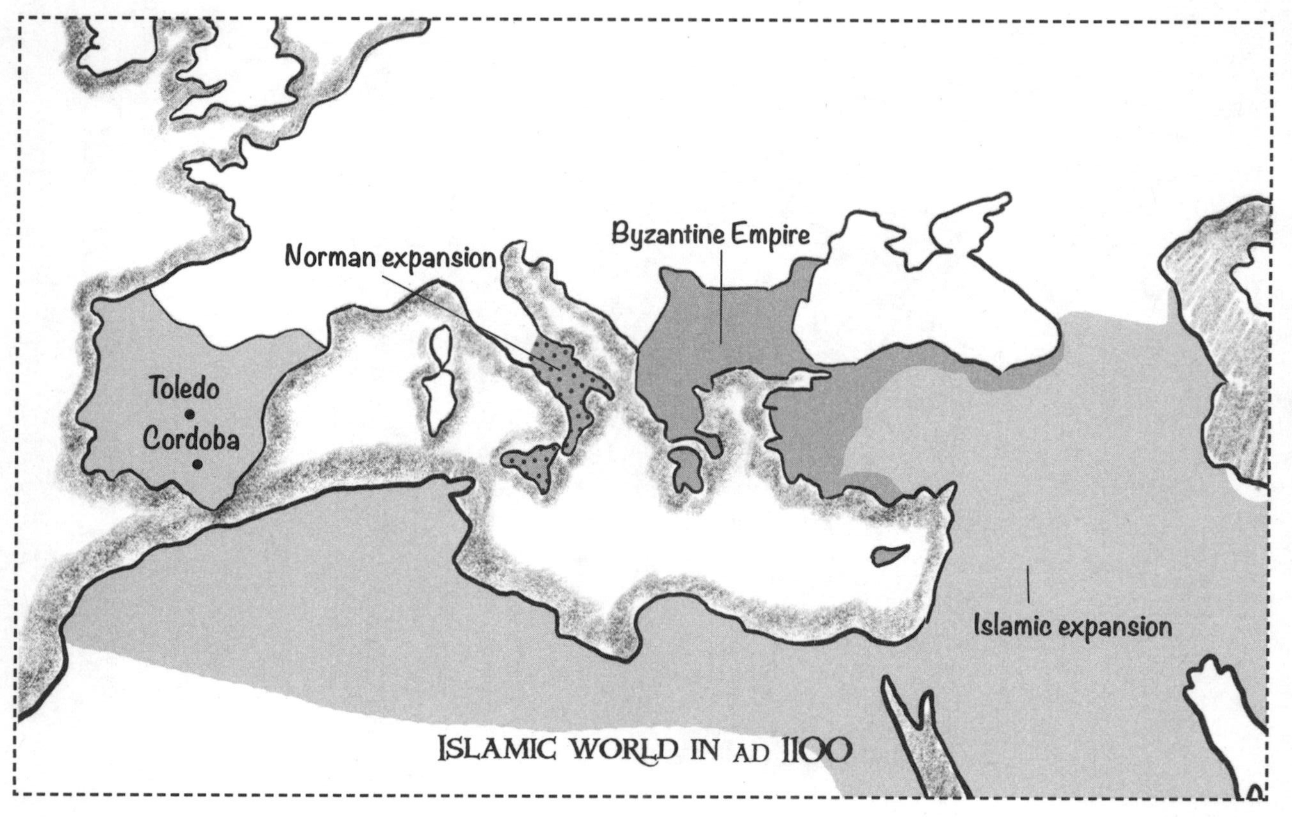

Norman expansion
Byzantine Empire
Toledo
Cordoba
Islamic expansion
ISLAMIC WORLD IN AD 1100

Milton studies it carefully. It looks very different from any map he has ever seen. "So Spain at this time is ruled by Muslim leaders?"

"That's right. They are called 'Moors' by historians. And they brought with them their scientists and books, as well as leaving behind some splendid buildings, like the Alhambra Palace in Granada. Our next stop is Toledo, in central Spain, but I wouldn't want you to miss out on other Islamic scientific highlights so I've prepared a little in-flight movie that you can watch while we travel."

Over in Persia, Al-Ghazali (1058–1111) stands up for science.

In Moorish Spain, Ibn Bajja (1095–1138), also known as Avempace, questions Aristotle's physics by repeating Philoponus' thoughts on impetus…

…before (possibly) being killed by a poisoned aubergine.

Only to have his (correct) challenge overthrown by Ibn Rushd, also know as Averroes (1226–1198), and Moses Maimoides (1135–1204).
TEAM ARISTOTLE
TEAM ARISTOTLE
But at least they were all talking about science!

The time machine lands and Milton rushes to the window.

"What can you see?" asks Harriet.

"We're in another courtyard, but this one is full of monks in long habits rather than turban-wearing scholars."

"Good. That means we've landed after the battle in 1085. Toledo has fallen to the King of Castile. All the books the Moorish rulers kept in the library here are now available to Christian scholars. As not many of them can read Arabic and few remember Greek, those who know those languages are in high demand as translators. We're off to take a peek at one of them, an Italian monk called Gerard of Cremona. He works alongside the Jewish and Muslim scholars who remain in Toledo in a new translation hub. We're just going to have a quick look at what he's up to as we have many other stops to make!"

"He is one of our key links," whispers Harriet. "Without Gerard – and without the heroes of the Islamic Golden Age – later scientists would have had to start from scratch without Greek thought."

Milton nibbles on a crust from Gerard's lunch box. The monk is too busy to notice. "I find it very interesting that scholars from Islam, Christianity, and Judaism are involved – they all must think very highly of learning," he observes.

Harriet pulls Milton away before he starts on the cheese. "And why do you think that is?"

"Because their big picture of the universe tells them to be curious about how God makes it work."

Harriet takes him back to the time machine. "Exactly. With that answer, I think, Milton, you're ready to go to university!"

Medieval Times: Good or Bad for Scientists?

Milton suddenly jumps over to the controls and puts his paw on the "stop" button.

"Me-ow! You don't mean you're taking me to medieval times, do you?"

Harriet tries to nudge him aside. "Milton, we're scooting about in the tenth century like a ball in a pinball machine. We have to input clear coordinates or we'll scramble the machine's computer."

"But Harriet," Milton exclaims, "there's no point! I know all about medieval science already."

"What do you know, Milton?"

"That there isn't any. They spent all their time debating silly things like how many angels dance on a pinhead and whether they would fall off the edge of a flat earth if they sailed too far west. Science didn't really get going until clever people – proper scientists – like Galileo came along."

LITTLE NOTE ON THE WORD "SCIENTIST"

We all know what scientists are, don't we? We do now, but the term was only invented in the nineteenth century. Before then people who studied what we now call science were usually called philosophers or natural philosophers. That was because scientific subjects weren't seen as separate from other subjects that asked questions, such as philosophy and theology.

Harriet tries to reach the buttons but Milton refuses to move. "I'm afraid that's just not right. That's what later writers said about medieval scholars to mock them. Most of the medieval thinkers know perfectly well that the earth is a sphere – they even know roughly the circumference of the globe. They are much more intelligent and much better scientists than you think."

"Oh." Milton is a bit miffed that Harriet always has to be right.

"You mustn't underestimate them. It's the age when scholars in Europe first start getting together to study – places that we call universities – which speeds up research because they are able to exchange ideas. That innovation has had a very long life and is where most science is done in our day, so we have to thank them for that at the very least."

"Humph!"

"And," Harriet continues, "we mustn't forget that it was the church that sponsors the setting up of universities – in fact most scientists at this time in Europe are monks. They are making some really exciting discoveries but unfortunately something big then gets in the way."

"What?" says Milton.

Harriet smiles. "Ah, you wait and see. I don't want to spoil the story. First we have some exciting new thinkers to visit. So, will you take your paw off the 'stop' button?"

Milton stalks away, a little kink at the end of his tail showing he is not happy. He has set ideas about medieval science and doesn't want to give them up without a fight. "I will, but you've got to prove they are good scientists – and I'm going to prove that they are bad ones!"

Harriet smiles to herself as she sets the machine running again. "You'll always find bad scientists in every era, Milton, but I look forward to hearing about some of your picks."

"Let's call it the Great Medieval Intelligence Test!" declares Milton, getting out a score card. "Where are we going to start?"

"Like I said: at university. Meanwhile, have a look at this timeline I prepared for you earlier."

SCIENCE IN MEDIEVAL EUROPE

c.1150 University of Paris established

1158 Founding of University of Bologna

c.1167 Beginning of University of Oxford

c.1174 Birth of Robert Grosseteste (Bighead) who, as head of Oxford University, went on to set out basics of the scientific method

1209 After riots in Oxford, some students flee to Cambridge and establish the university

1209 Disturbances in Paris result in Bishop of Paris banning the teaching of Aristotle

c.1220 Birth of Roger Bacon, pioneer in the study of nature through the scientific method

1285 Birth of William of Ockham, famous for the problem-solving idea called Ockham's razor

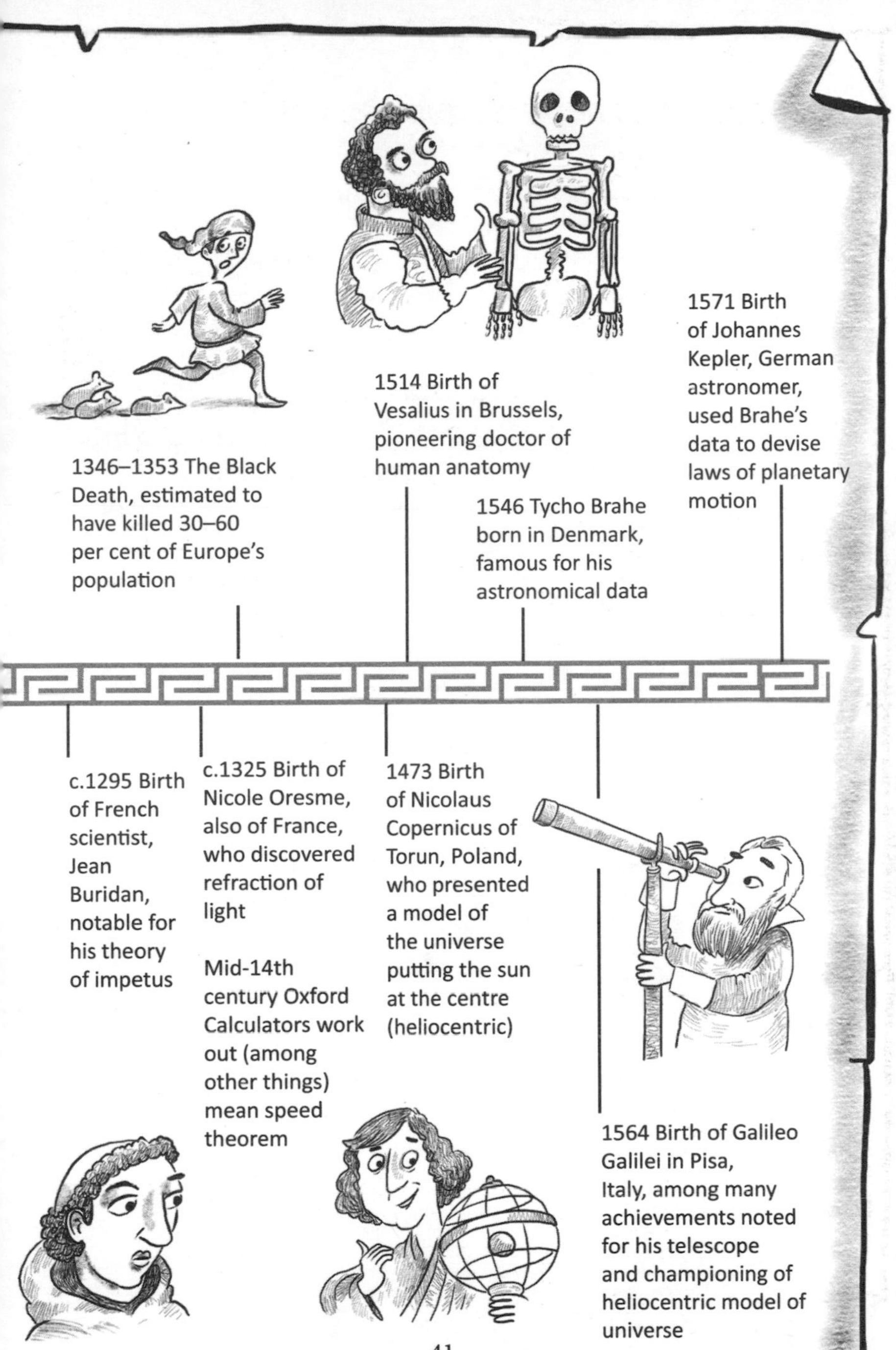
1346–1353 The Black Death, estimated to have killed 30–60 per cent of Europe's population
1514 Birth of Vesalius in Brussels, pioneering doctor of human anatomy
1546 Tycho Brahe born in Denmark, famous for his astronomical data
1571 Birth of Johannes Kepler, German astronomer, used Brahe's data to devise laws of planetary motion
c.1295 Birth of French scientist, Jean Buridan, notable for his theory of impetus
c.1325 Birth of Nicole Oresme, also of France, who discovered refraction of light
Mid-14th century Oxford Calculators work out (among other things) mean speed theorem
1473 Birth of Nicolaus Copernicus of Torun, Poland, who presented a model of the universe putting the sun at the centre (heliocentric)
1564 Birth of Galileo Galilei in Pisa, Italy, among many achievements noted for his telescope and championing of heliocentric model of universe

GERBERT THE MATHEMATICAL POPE AND THE MYSTERIOUS BRASS HEAD

One of the interesting characters in the early days of medieval science is a monk called Gerbert, who became the Mathematical Pope. He was tutor to the Holy Roman Emperor, Otto III, and was made Pope in 999 by his former pupil. He made a mediocre pope but was an excellent scholar. Thanks to training in Arabic science when he lived for a while in Spain, he introduced Indian numbers to the West, a link in the chain that means you do your maths using numbers 0 to 9 rather than Roman numerals.

But he is also worth a look because of an extraordinary story that grew up about him. He was so clever that one writer, William of Malmesbury, claims he got all his knowledge from a talking brass head.

Watch out for the return of the brass head. We've not finished with it yet!

The time machine lands in a dark corner of a covered walkway surrounding a garden on four sides. Milton pokes his head outside and sniffs.

"I can smell smoke, drains, and a river. Where are we?"

"Oxford, in 1209. We will be shuttling between here and Paris for the next steps on our quest," says Harriet.

Milton steps onto the pavement. "Ah, this is more like it: a quiet cloister, scholars beavering away in libraries, everything peaceful so learning can advance!"

Just then two men run through the college and disappear out of sight. They are pursued by a host of angry locals.

"Get the scholars!" cries one, a call that is taken up by everyone in the crowd.

"Harriet, what's going on?" asks Milton, nipping back into the safety of the time machine. She (very wisely) has stayed inside.

"You're witnessing the riot that causes the founding of another university. Two scholars are wrongly blamed for a crime committed by a friend and, I'm sorry to say, they are killed by the townsfolk. The mood in Oxford is so ugly that the surviving scholars worry that they will be next. They flee and set up in another place – Cambridge. Scholars don't return to Oxford until 1214 when the townsfolk are punished and the university is allowed to carry on (with more protection for its members)."

Milton scratches his ear. "What's that got to do with science?"

Harriet checks the onscreen map of the world. "I wanted you to see that, just as with the Greeks, sometimes learning spreads because it is forced to move by those who distrust it. The local people think the clever men in the colleges get away with treating them badly so take revenge – but on the people."

Milton looks out of the porthole, not liking the flames he can see blazing over the rooftops. "Like the men of Athens did to Socrates?"

"Exactly," says Harriet. "Let's go to Paris – same year."

"I hope it's nice and peaceful…"

"Ah." Harriet is being very cagey.

They arrive in the French capital, only to find that it is also in the middle of a riot. Scholars are fleeing the city

"Harriet, what's going on here? Another crime?" asks Milton, giving up his idea of having a quiet supper of snails by the Seine as ten scholars are herded away to be executed near the city gates.

"Only the crime of thinking what some leaders at this time regard as forbidden thoughts," explains Harriet. "The Bishop of Paris believes that the scholars have fallen into bad ways because they studied too much Aristotle. Some have been saying things like 'all things are God' – which to the bishop is against the message of their faith. As a result, I'm afraid some are executed and Aristotle's works are banned from the teaching curriculum. That ban isn't removed until 1231 under a new pope. It's another example of new thinking shaking up society in ways which make people very uncomfortable."

Milton is not enjoying all this bad news. "You're not convincing me that medieval people were good scientists – rather the opposite! Riots and bans – we're going backwards, not forwards!"

"I'm just laying out the background," says Harriet. "Let's go back to Oxford. Science is about to make better progress."

"Is it safe?"

"Oh yes. We are going after 1214 to visit the university's first chancellor, Robert Bighead."

Milton cheers up on hearing the silly name. "That's what he is called? Really?"

"Oh yes. He is about to finish an experiment."

"That's more like it!"

"An experiment about what makes you throw up red bile."

"Harriet! That's yucky!"

Harriet laughs. "I know: science isn't always pretty."

Fortunately they arrive in Robert's study after he has conducted his experiment with scammony, a plant that is known to produce a purging effect (that means it makes you sick). He is looking a little green but also very pleased with himself. He mutters as he writes. "So by repeating the test, I observe that scammony does produce red bile each time. From these results, I can work out a universal principle."

"See," whispers Harriet, "he's using a method that modern scientists would recognize: testing out an idea to see if the same outcome is produced each time."

Robert starts holding pieces of glass in a range of hues up to the light.

"What's he doing now?" whispers Milton.

"He thinks that, as light is part of the physical world, then a scientist can understand it in physical terms," explains Harriet. "That's important to scientists who we'll meet later. He also thinks you can use lenses to see things far away and close up. His ideas have to wait for instrument makers to catch up and make that possible, but he is right. He also describes mathematics as a central part of God's creation, echoing ideas we heard in Greece and Baghdad. So do you still think medieval scientists aren't very good?"

Milton sniffs and produces a page from his notebook with a flourish. "I've been doing my own research and I offer my first counter example."

MILTON'S NOTEBOOK OF (MOSTLY) WRONG IDEAS NUMBER 1

ADELARD OF BATH c. 1080–c. 1160

The Medievals did debate some odd things despite whatever Harriet says. In trying to answer questions posed by his nephew, Adelard of Bath came up with some ingenious but mostly wrong answers.

Explaining why oceans don't overflow with all the water running into them, he suggested that it is recycled by underground streams that emerge as springs on land.

He also suggested that because stars moved they had to be living things. That in turn meant they had souls and had to eat. He thought the most likely food was the air rising from the earth.

P.S. He did, however, play an important part in the advance of science when he translated Euclid's *Elements* for a Western audience from an Arabic version so he gets a pat on the back for that.

Harriet hands back the note about Adelard. "I think you're being a bit hard on poor Adelard. His answers make the best sense of the world as he knows it by sticking to the rules of rational enquiry. In his world picture, the way to do science is to reason his way to an answer rather than run an experiment to test a theory as we would do. This is what many of his fellow thinkers do too. They are called Scholastics by historians."

"You're just making excuses for Adelard," protests Milton. "Thinking about things doesn't get you very far – and takes you down lots of blind alleys!"

"That's why people like Robert Bighead are so special – they move science on from reasoning to experimenting. Now I think you need to meet a man nicknamed the Dumb Ox."

Milton doesn't get up from where he is comfortably curled up on the control desk. "You're not selling him to me, Harriet."

She chuckles. "I know. He's really called Thomas Aquinas. He's the son of an Italian nobleman and he goes to Paris in 1245 to learn from a man called Albert the Great. Albert said that the dumb ox is so good a thinker that all Europe will hear his bellow – and he was right."

Milton licks a paw. "And what's so great about Albert? He sounds like he should be called 'big head' too!"

"For one, he spots a talent in the young Italian and asks Aquinas to take on the biggest challenge of the day: how to reconcile top ancient science expert, Aristotle, with the beliefs of Christianity – it was really making people hot under the collar as you saw with the riots."

"Don't remind me. I never got my snails," sighs Milton.

"But we do have a brass head alert!"

"Oh, I like those!"

"Albert is so knowledgeable they say… guess what, Milton?"

"That he gets all his answers from the handy brass head last seen with Gerbert the Mathematical Pope?" guesses Milton.

Harriet smiles. "Got it in one! His best idea though was to let Aquinas loose on Aristotle's works."

SPRINGTIME IN PARIS

Milton and Harriet arrive at the University of Paris to catch the end of Aquinas' lecture. They wriggle their way through the crowd of attentive listeners, managing to get right up to the front. He is lecturing in a courtyard filled with blossom blown there from nearby trees.

"Trees produce blossom, the blossom fruit, the fruit seed, leading to more trees. You see, my brothers," says Aquinas, leaning over the edge of the pulpit, "there is no effect without a cause, so by reason we must look for a first cause outside our universe. God created the laws of nature but is not bound by them. He is outside it, like Aristotle's prime mover."

"Harriet, Harriet," Milton whispers excitedly, "he is talking about what came first, just like the Greeks did!"

"I know," she replies. "It's an excellent big question, isn't it? But it leads to really interesting follow up ones that encourage science to develop. Here's one now."

A hand goes up just behind Milton. "But Aristotle said the universe was eternal – that there was no moment of creation."

Aquinas nods. "And I think he was wrong on that point. You must not be afraid, brother, to question his findings, no matter how formidable his reputation. You must think for yourself!" A bell tolls, marking the end of the lesson. The crowd breaks up.

"You see what he did there?" asks Harriet.

"Let them all go home for lunch? I'm a bit peckish myself. We haven't eaten since the Islamic Golden Age." Milton's mouth is watering at the thought.

"Not that!" says Harriet. "I meant Aquinas cleared the way so that scholars in places like this university were convinced that reason could exist with their faith. In fact, he shows you *can* use reason to find arguments for God's existence."

"So in that case, is it reasonable to suggest it is lunchtime?" asks Milton. "I can make some very good arguments that it is, like the one that my stomach is rumbling."

Harriet sighs. Milton's curiosity is at a low ebb at the moment. "You're missing the step forward, Milton. Aquinas also allows them to question great minds of the past like Aristotle. If you are too daunted to question whether the Greek's model of the universe is right, you won't look for the evidence that challenges it. Aquinas gives them the courage to think outside the Aristotle box!"

"Shall we get back in our box? I think I left a sardine sandwich in there." Milton is already heading back to the time machine.

Harriet gives up, deciding she'd better wait until after lunch to carry on the Curiosity Quest. "Oh all right. After you've eaten, I want to introduce you to a friend of Robert Bighead. His name is Friar Bacon."

Milton stops short, still thinking about food. "Did you say you were going to take me to a man who will fry me some bacon?"

"Do pay attention, Milton!" Harriet scolds. "We are going to meet a man called Friar Roger Bacon. He's another Oxford scholar, but he can sometimes be found in Paris."

Feeling a little grumpy, Milton follows in her footsteps. "How can I be expected to pay attention when I'm hungry?" His eyes brighten as an idea strikes him. "So the cause of my hunger is not having eaten, see? Aquinas is right: every effect must have a cause. If I eat, then the effect will be a lovely feeling of fullness – and that in turn will cause me to be very intelligent when we make our next stop." He walks with a little flick at the end of his tail, proving that he feels very pleased with himself already.

Harriet has to laugh. "So you were listening to Aquinas! I suggest you eat your sandwich before we get to Friar Bacon's study. You don't want to miss this next step in the quest."

A TECHNICAL INTERLUDE: RICHARD OF WALLINGFORD AND THE FIRST SMART WATCH

Who invented the first smart watch, long before Apple and Android got in on the act?

To answer this we must stop by Richard of Wallingford (1292–1336). He rose from humble origins to be an abbot. He studied at Oxford and went on to invent the first smart watch. (OK, it was really a clock in St Alban's abbey but telling the time was the least of what it could do.) He must have been a brilliant mathematician because the mechanism was full of what we would now call apps. For example, it told you the state of the tides at London Bridge and it doubled as an astrolabe (star measurer). The world hadn't seen anything like it before.

Mechanical clocks like this were new and they also brought about the invention of what we think of as standard time. It was an unnamed clockmaker in Padua in the 1340s who decided that, for example, the hours should be counted from midnight to midday. No longer were workers governed by daylight, working longer in summer than winter; they now had a fixed number of hours set by a machine.

I bet yours doesn't tell you when your ship can set sail.

MEDIEVAL TECH

Medieval people certainly weren't backward when it came to adopting new technologies. Here are just some of the things they introduced, many of which came down the trade route, known as the Silk Road, from China:

- compass
- paper
- printing
- stirrups
- gunpowder
- an improved plough (it turned the earth over)

And here are just a few of the things invented in the West:

- spectacles
- mechanical clock
- European windmill
- an early form of blast furnace

Putting Roger Bacon to the Test

The time machine is taking the scenic route to Friar Bacon's study in 1266 to give our travellers time to digest. Sandwiches eaten, Milton is ready to challenge Harriet again in the Great Medieval Intelligence Test.

"You were impressed by Aquinas, weren't you?" Milton asks Harriet as she nibbles her dandelion leaf.

"Oh yes."

"But you have to admit, he and his fellow scholars could also spend their time doing very foolish things. I've compiled a list." He presents it to her with a flourish.

MILTON'S NOTEBOOK OF (MOSTLY) WRONG IDEAS 2

SILLY STUDIES IN MEDIEVAL TIMES – MILTON'S TOP DEBATES

I think Harriet is pretending the scholars were all very sensible but in fact they had some very silly ideas. My research shows that using reason to puzzle the way to an answer (Scholasticism) led to some very odd questions being debated. The questions often mixed up scientific ideas with theological ones. Real questions they spent ages debating have survived. They include:

- "If a person was born with two heads, should they be baptized as one or two people?" The underlying question here is biological – is it a head that makes a person? – as well as the theological one of how many souls they have.
- "If a bishop is raised from the dead, can he get his job back?"
- "Is it better for a crusader to die on the way to the Holy Land or on the way back?"

P.S. Before Harriet says it, I now know that one question they don't appear to have debated is the one for which they are most famous: "how many angels can dance on a pinhead?" This was invented as a joke about Aquinas centuries later.

Harriet reads the list carefully.

"So they weren't all super clever like you say," says Milton, feeling he has at last scored a point. "They were running up all sorts of blind alleys."

"Have you ever been in a school debate, Milton?"

"I sat on someone's knee for one."

"You'll remember then that they always pose a question like 'This house believes that cereal is better than toast for breakfast' and then the two sides have to argue for and against?"

"Yes," says Milton warily.

"It's a form of entertainment."

"Agreed – though everyone knows fish makes the best breakfast."

"But it also trains the people taking part to think."

Milton doesn't say anything as he can see where she is going with this.

"These medieval questions may sound silly but they were really meant as a chance for the best debaters to show off their talents. The scholars enjoyed it. It doesn't really tell us much about the state of science, other than that reason is highly valued. To find out what was going on, we need to..."

"Fry bacon?"

"Yes. And we are here." Harriet peers out of the porthole. "By the way, we have a brass head alert!"

"Don't tell me they thought Friar Bacon had the head too! It's like a great game of pass the parcel. Who gets it when the music stops?"

"The same Friar Bacon, because it ends its legendary journey with him. The story says he made it into the door knocker that gave its name to Brasenose (or Brass Nose) College, Oxford, and can still be seen in our time."

Milton trots after her. "Knock, knock."

"Who's there?"

"Noah."

"Noah who?"

"Noah a good place to find out about science?"

Chuckling together, they step out of the time machine and into Friar Bacon's study on Folly Bridge in Oxford. He is busy poring over a map of the world with a magnifying lens in his hand.

"Oh hello: where on earth did you come from?" he asks when he notices Milton's tail snaking across his map. "Be careful, Puss: I'm sending this map and my book to the Pope."

"We are travellers," says Harriet, deciding to avoid mentioning time travel. "We were told you have some very interesting ideas about studying nature."

Pleased by her compliment, Friar Bacon invites them to join him by his fireside for a drink and a snack of cheese and bread. "I believe that all truth, wherever it is found, belongs to Christ, including the truths of nature."

"So how do you go about it?" asks Milton.

"I have two tools. One: the knowledge of languages that enables me to read the writings of the great minds of the past; two: mathematics!"

Milton's ears prick up. He has already decided that he really has to polish up on his maths. Every scientist from the Greeks onwards seems to think it vital.

"And then what do you do?" asks Harriet.

"There are two ways in which we can know things. We either have experience of things spiritual – that's what happens inside us; or we can look at the experience gained through our external senses, which I term the science of experiment."

Milton's whiskers twitch with excitement. "Now we're getting somewhere," he whispers.

Harriet gives him a warning look not to alarm the friar with his enthusiasm. "How do you go about that?" Even Harriet's voice is a little higher than usual as she shares Milton's eagerness.

"Well, take this drop of water." Friar Bacon dribbles a little onto Milton's paw. "Hold it up to the light. See: it contains the same colours as you see in a rainbow?"

"Yes, we see," agrees Milton.

"I've made a number of tests and I've found that a rainbow doesn't appear in the sky above an elevation of 42°. I think that there is a connection between the laws of light refraction and the rainbow. It is by experimentation, not reasoning, that I have come to that conclusion. My brothers out there," he gestures to the busy world beyond his window, "are too often reliant on puzzling things out for themselves without testing against experience."

"And do you think the Pope will like your book?" Harriet asks delicately.

He shakes his head. "I don't know, little tortoise. I seem to fall in and out of favour depending on what is happening in politics. They are worried that a big new idea will cause riots, as it did in 1209, and has done many times since. But I'm not worried: once my ideas are in the library, others can read and make up their own mind about them. My time will come. The science of experiment is a method that will prove its worth."

"I think you're right there." Harriet gives Milton a sly wink. "Thank you so much, Friar Bacon, for showing us your rainbow droplet."

"Can I help you with anything else? I don't get many visitors as the Church Fathers are trying to keep me quiet."

Milton knows this is his only chance. "There is one thing before we go."

"Oh yes?"

"Can you show me your brass head?"

"You mean the one that gives me all my best ideas?"

"That's the one!"

The friar laughs. "Here it is." He taps his own head. "That's where my ideas come from. It isn't so remarkable really once you stop and think. We all have a brain."

Milton trails after Harriet as she gets back in the time machine. Just as the door closes, he catches a glimpse of the friar taking a cover off a brazen head that has been hidden under the map… "Harriet!"

"Don't ask," warns Harriet. "Some stories are best left as a mystery."

WHAT DID PEOPLE ONCE THINK OF AS "SCIENCE"?

Science wasn't a term used in this era, but if you look at what serious scholars, people like Roger Bacon, were investigating you find some surprising subjects included in the curriculum. In addition to mathematics, medicine, and astronomy, the most important subjects were:

Astrology – people believed they could tell many things from patterns in the stars. The good news for science was that this encouraged the study of mathematics to work out the star positions and also led to advances in astronomy, such as the discovery that the earth goes round the sun.

Alchemy – many scholars were seeking for ways to turn base metals to gold and to find the secret to eternal life. Some thought the legendary philosopher's stone held the key. There is, of course, no such substance but by searching for it they did science some good by encouraging enquiry into the nature of the elements. That was to become what we call chemistry.

MEET THE SCIENTIST

WILLIAM OF OCKHAM
A MEDIEVAL SHERLOCK HOLMES!

- Lived: 1287-1347 AD
- Number of jobs: 2 (philosopher and theologian)
- Influence (out of 100): 70 – for Ockham's razor
- Right? (out of 20): 10 – Ockham's razor had a largely positive effect
- Helpfully wrong? (out of 10): 5 – a balance. Against the helpful razor was his view that human reason would never be able to understand the world or God. Some took this as an argument to give up seeking answers
- Interesting fact: William was a rebel. He was excommunicated (that means he was thrown out of the church) by the Pope in 1328 for leaving town without permission

William was a Franciscan monk studying in Oxford. He had an idea that is still used today and is known as "Ockham's razor". It states that when looking at rival theories, the one that makes the fewest assumptions should be selected. In short – don't go for the complicated solution if there's a simple one available!

That's what we expect the detective Sherlock Holmes to say.

THE ROAD GETS ROCKY: NEW IDEAS AND THE BLACK DEATH

"So Harriet, where are we going now?" says Milton, checking her timeline. "Somewhere sunny like Italy?"

"Not yet. We're staying in Oxford, but going forward to 1348. We're visiting the dream team: the Merton Calculators."

"Me-ow, they had calculators back then!"

Harriet rolls her eyes. "Not that sort of calculator. I mean a group of brilliant mathematicians: Thomas Bradwardine, Richard Swineshead, and William of Heytesbury. They all are gathered in Merton College. Let's go and eavesdrop on them."

MEET THE DREAM TEAM!

Playing up front is Brainy Bradwardine. Oh, would you look at that! He hits the post with his formula for a falling object!
Smartie Swineshead moves in to support him with backup calculations.
GOAL! Handy Heytesbury comes up with a formula for working out mean speed.
And that's a victory for science as maths and physics are used together for the first time.

Harriet and Milton watch the three men discussing their ideas in Merton's library.

"Why is Brainy Bradwardine's formula only a near miss?" whispers Milton.

"Because his calculations are for an object moving according to Aristotle's picture of the universe – and we already know that is wrong, thanks to John Philoponus of Alexandria. Aristotle thinks a heavier body falls faster than a lighter one. The maths is right but the physics wrong."

"And Smartie Swineshead?"

"He made a book of calculations based on his friend's work."

"And the third?"

"Handy Heytesbury is right on target. You can still use his formula today. Their method of combining maths and physics spreads across Europe, as we'll see." Harriet waves goodbye to the Oxford scholars and heads back to the time machine. "But that's it from England for two centuries. The action moves back to Paris."

TRY THIS AT HOME

Want to become part of the dream team of Merton Calculators? Why not try out William of Heytesbury's formula to work out mean speed?

He puts it like this:

"A moving body will travel in an equal period of time, a distance exactly equal to that which it would travel if it were moving continuously at its mean speed."

Milton got confused when he read that so he needs your help. It's easier to understand when you try it out. The idea is you can work out the mean speed an object has travelled if you know the time taken and the distance.

So imagine a farmer is plodding along in her cart heading for market. She travels 4 miles and after one hour arrives at the market. Her mean speed is 4 miles per hour. Easy, huh?

But, half an hour after the farmer set off, a knight on his charger starts from the same village and goes along the same road. He spurs his horse to go faster and faster. Knight and horse arrive at the same time as the farmer.

What is the knight's mean speed?

8 miles per hour: he travelled 4 miles in 30 minutes.

The time machine brings them to the banks of the River Seine in Paris. It's a sunny day in 1348 and many Parisians are heading out into the countryside for picnics.

The scientist, Jean Buridan,

is here, announces the time machine, enjoying his day of rest.

"That's our man over there: quick!" Harriet says, moving as fast as she can towards a rowing boat. "Let's see if he'll take us along with him. Excuse me, sir!"

The scholar looks up from his rowing bench. "Good gracious! Who are you two?"

"We're travellers. I know it is odd that we talk but you'll soon get used to us."

"You can tell yourself you're dreaming if you like," suggests Milton.

"I see. I might just do that." Jean beckons them closer. "Can I help you?"

"We were wondering if we could come along with you and talk about your ideas?" asks Harriet.

"My pleasure. Let me lift you down."

When they are settled, Jean starts rowing. "I can't tell you how good it is to get away from my study. I'm meeting my friend Nicole Oresme. We like to look at nature together, see what we can learn from the world."

"And what have you learned?" asks Milton, sniffing the picnic basket.

"For one, that Aristotle got things wrong." Jean points to some children playing on archery butts in an orchard. "Take an arrow in flight. I think that it has some quality that I have called *impetus*, or motion, within itself from the bow, and is slowed down as the air resists. In a vacuum, with no counter force, an arrow could in theory travel on forever."

Harriet winks at Milton. "I think you might be right."

"My idea is that an all-powerful God gives the world a single law of motion, so you could even expand the idea from an arrow to the movement of planets."

"Think big: yes, that's exciting," agrees Milton. "So what would it mean?"

Jean pulls hard at the oars as they go past a fishing boat. "That maybe it is the world that spins in space, not the heavens around the earth, despite the fact that it looks like that when we stargaze."

"What do you mean?"

"Take that fisherman in the boat we've just passed. Imagine it is night and we both have candles. Neither of us could be sure which one was moving. The fisherman would see us getting further away but he won't know if he is still or if he is moving unless he can see the shore. That is because he has nothing against which to judge his own movement. Maybe that is why we think the heavens move – it's a kind of illusion.

"Ah, there's Nicole." Jean heads for the shore.

"I like the way this man thinks," whispers Milton to Harriet.

"He's also an exception because, unlike almost everyone else we've met from these times, he didn't train as a theologian or join a monastic order. Yet that doesn't stop him becoming head of the university."

"Nicole!" calls Jean. "Let me introduce you to two very unusual travellers. They were asking about my ideas of motion. I expect they might like to hear yours."

Nicole helps Jean beach the boat and they spread out a picnic blanket on the grass. Milton settles down on a sunny patch thinking this is quite the nicest adventure he's had in Paris. So much better than the riot over a century ago.

"I think," he says, "that if we accept Jean's idea that the earth spins, then the reason why an arrow shot into the air moves away from the archer rather than relative to the moving earth is that it shares the same atmosphere. The arrow, the archer and the earth are all moving together. A simpler way of showing this is: if you jump you land on the same spot, not several paces away as you would if the world spun without you being in contact with it. Mind you, I don't think I can prove the earth moves like this, so I might be wrong."

Milton is about to reassure him that he is correct but Harriet steps on his tail.

"Don't!" she whispers. "Nicole does back away from the idea but he's done enough questioning so that later scientists take it up and prove it."

Encouraged by the interest of two extraordinary visitors, Nicole produces a sketch from his bag. "Do you want to see my graph for mean speed? I picked up the idea from the Merton Calculators but thought this would be a good way of showing it."

Harriet and Milton peer at it closely. Milton thinks it looks like a piece of cheese. He tries licking it.

"Stop that. This might just be the first graph ever!" she tells him.

"Yes, nature is a wonderful thing," says Nicole, paddling his toes in the cool water. He fortunately doesn't notice Milton's attempts to eat his diagram. "When I see that movement follows a consistent rule and can be plotted reliably on a graph, it makes me think that God made the heavens like a clock which he winds up and leaves to run down by motion all of its own."

Harriet nudges Milton. "He might be the first, but he certainly isn't the last to make that clock comparison."

As the two scholars snooze in the sunshine, Milton's whiskers prick up. He has just caught the smell of a rat leaving a ship moored by the dock. His hunting instincts are alerted.

"I'm just going to stretch my legs," he tells Harriet.

Knowing his ways, she blocks his exit. "No, you can't. Not now."

"Why not? There's a rat. I'm a cat. It's my job to catch it. It's the natural way of things."

"Not today. There's something I've not been telling you."

"Uh-oh."

"Yes, it is the biggest uh-oh moment of them all. We'd better slip away and return to the time machine. I'll tell you the bad news as we go back."

They hitch a ride on a barge heading into Paris.

"What do I need to know?"

"Rattus rattus."

"Bless you."

"I'm not sneezing. It's the Latin for black rats. Their fleas bring bubonic plague to Italy on ships fleeing war in the east. From 1348 and for the next fifty years about a third to a half of the population of Europe dies."

"Oh, Harriet, that's terrible! You mean all these people enjoying the sunshine might soon die?"

"I know. Tragic for the people but also tragic for the science quest. The scholars were really just getting going and then Brainy Bradwardine dies of plague, and we think Jean Buridan does too. Society takes a huge knock; literacy rates plunge as time can't be spared for education; and many years pass before people recover."

Milton gets back into the time machine, whiskers drooping. "Poor Jean. Poor medieval people."

Harriet sets about fumigating them both in case they picked up any fleas during their visit. "Think of him enjoying his sunny picnic. He achieved a lot even if his life was cut short. It's time for us to jump ahead and rejoin the science quest at the Renaissance."

Book a Place in History: Gutenberg, Copernicus, and Kepler

"So what's a renaissance?" asks Milton as the time machine spins them forward on their quest. Milton is feeling restless after his close encounter with the plague. Twitching from side to side, his tail brushes over the controls.

Harriet scowls and adjusts the dial he has touched. "No no, too early for America. We don't want to go there yet. Milton, mind what you do with that tail!"

Milton sighs. "Harriet?"

Harriet is looking harassed as she puts his mistake right. "The word is French and it means to be born again, or rebirth."

"Rebirth of what?"

"Everything – art, philosophy, science, religion. The historians who came up with the name had a big picture of the world where they thought that the medieval period had killed off the scientific and cultural advances made by the Greeks. They believed Europe needed a new start to get back on track."

"This I have to see, Harriet. A whole new start. So where are we going?" Milton peeks out of the porthole to see if he can get a clue. Bell towers, palaces, and churches spin past. "I can't wait to find out more."

His enthusiasm cheers Harriet. She too has been fretting over the horrible time of the plague. "There's a lot to pick from the Renaissance as it refers to a period from roughly the fifteenth century to the early seventeenth." Harriet points to the timeline.

"I was hoping you would help me decide where we land."

Milton suddenly realizes something is wrong. He nudges her front foot away from the control pad. "Before we do that – you said the historians claim the medieval period was a step backwards?"

"That's right. Some scholars until recently even called the earlier part, the time of the Anglo-Saxons and Vikings, 'the Dark Ages' – as if the lights had gone out for learning all over Europe."

"What about the Merton Calculators in Oxford, and Jean Buridan in Paris, not to mention the Islamic Golden Age in Spain and elsewhere, which started during the so-called Dark Ages?"

Harriet smiles. "Exactly, Milton, but the idea lingers. Even you fell for it. What was it you said about the medieval thinkers being bad scientists?"

"Harriet, that is awfully close to an 'I told you so.'"

"But you've got the right idea now. The Renaissance thinkers were using the work of those that came before even if they didn't acknowledge the debt. But it is also true there was a new flourishing across Europe, like crops springing up from seeds that had been planted by these earlier scholars. I've another timeline for you."

"Excellent!"

SCIENCE IN THE RENAISSANCE

1453 Fall of Constantinople, end of the Byzantine Empire

1455 First books printed on the Gutenberg press, bringing in a new age of the spread of information

1473 Birth of Nicolaus Copernicus, astronomer

1492 Columbus discovers America

1514 Birth of famous doctor, Vesalius, in Brussels. His dissections and later writings go on to correct many of the wrong ideas about the human body inherited from classical writers

1522 Magellan completes first circumnavigation of the globe

1541 Birth of Tycho Brahe, astronomer

1543 Vesalius's book on the human body and Copernicus's book on the revolution of the planets both published in this year

1561 Birth of Francis Bacon

1564 Birth of Galileo Galilei in Pisa; Shakespeare born in Stratford, England

1571 Birth of Johannes Kepler, who went on to devise his three laws of planetary motion

1572 Arrival of “Tycho’s Star”, a supernova that blazed for 18 months. As it clearly took place beyond the moon, it caused many to question Aristotle’s claim that the heavens were unchanging

1608 Telescope invented in the Netherlands; the following year Galileo improves upon the design and turns it to the heavens

1616 Galileo warned not to teach Copernican hypothesis

1628 William Harvey publishes a book showing that the blood circulates

1632 Galileo publishes his book, *Dialogue on the Two Chief World Systems*

1633 Galileo found guilty of heresy and placed under house arrest. His works continue to be published abroad, including new ones

"With that in mind, where shall we go first? Italy or Germany?"

"That's like asking 'ice cream or sausages?' I like both."

"Milton!"

Milton struggles to remain on track when distracted once more by the idea of food. "Well, this is a science quest. What's the most important change for science?"

"I think I have an idea what that is." Getting out a note, Harriet enters coordinates for a destination but doesn't let him see what she is doing. She slips the piece of paper under her shell.

"Where are we going?" asks Milton.

"You have to guess. Your clue is that it's a very *impressive* place."

Milton quickly thinks through the list of cities Harriet might find awesome, putting to the top the ones where he stands the chance of getting the best ice cream. "Rome? Florence? Paris?"

"No." Harriet is looking incredibly smug. Milton drags his mind away from a double scoop chocolate chip swirl with cherries and realizes the hint is in the word "impressive". An idea drops into his mind as he recalls the many libraries they have visited on their quest.

"Ah, I know! The printing press!" He claps his paws.

Harriet taps on the landing button. "All right, clever clogs, it's Germany first. Let's go to Gutenberg Press in 1455 and see the first book come off the printing machine."

BIG GUNS, LITTLE GUNS, AND IMPERIAL SOCKS

Harriet and Milton don't have time to visit every significant event on their quest, but while they head for Germany we're going to call in on the fall of Byzantium in 1453.

First, though, we have to make a quick visit back in time. Towards the end of the Roman Empire in 330, the Emperor Constantine founded a new city in the East, and modestly named it after himself: Constantinople (present-day Istanbul). When the last Roman emperor abdicated in 476, much of the culture of the old empire was preserved in this new capital.

Fast forward to 1453 and Constantinople is under siege from the new Ottoman Sultan Mehmet II. The city was famous for its impenetrable walls but the sultan had a new technology to help him, thanks to a Hungarian engineer called Urban. Urban built huge cannon for the Sultan's army. These battered down the walls and the city was taken. The last Byzantine emperor lost his head (literally) in the attack and was only identified after the battle by the imperial badge on his socks.

The irony was that the Ottoman troops were able to take the city due to European technology developed for the crusades.

Engineers were also busy working on small arms and by 1500 the matchlock musket had been invented. This meant that over the next few centuries Europeans could beat any nation they came up against as long as they didn't have muskets too. Chinese gunpowder technology had been turned in the West to deadly advantage.

Harriet and Milton emerge from the time machine on a street in Mainz, Germany. The houses are colourful – white, yellow, and dark red – with grey tiled roofs. For a city of the fifteenth century is seems very tidy and prosperous. Milton's ears prick up: he can already smell something odd in the air and a booming sound rolls out along the street at regular intervals.

Harriet doesn't seem worried though. She is already trotting towards a shop on the other side of the road. "One thing to know about Germany, Milton, is that at this time the country is divided into lots of little states."

"But they still all have sausages?" asks Milton.

"Yes, I think I can promise you that."

They enter the shop. A man is guiding his apprentices through the painstaking process of placing metal type into rows. Each little piece of type has a different letter formed backwards on it.

"What are they doing?" whispers Milton.

"This is where the printing starts. See those pages of handwriting over there? The men are copying the text onto the composing sticks to form words."

"But why are they backwards?"

"Think about it. It has to be that way so that when you ink it and press down, the word will then be printed to read the right way."

TRY THIS AT HOME: MAKE YOUR OWN GUTENBERG POTATO PRESS!

Have a go at a simple form of printing to see the reverse type in action. Always take care when doing experiments. This one uses a vegetable knife and a potato so make sure you have permission before you start. First write your initials backwards on a piece of scrap paper (you can use a mirror to check you are getting it right). Now take a large potato and slice it in half. Dry the exposed surface with a piece of kitchen towel. Carefully carve your backwards initials into the fleshy part with a vegetable knife, or ask an adult to do it for you. Cover the surface evenly with poster paint – not too thick or your print will smudge – and then wipe the paint off the flat parts with a straight edge. Now stamp your potato press onto a clean sheet of paper. Lift it up.

Did your initials come out right?

What other designs can you make with the other half of the potato?

"This is one of Gutenberg's major discoveries," continues Harriet. "Chinese printers had invented their own form of press but as their language works differently, they didn't have this option of endlessly combining twenty-six letters into new words. The alphabet made printing much more economical and adaptable."

"What else did Gutenberg do?" asks Milton.

Unfortunately, it is at that moment the printer catches sight of the pair of time travellers. He doesn't take kindly to their sudden arrival in his workroom. "What are you two doing in my shop? Are you spying for my rivals?" bellows Johannes Gutenberg, grabbing a broom from the corner.

"Let me handle this," whispers Milton to Harriet. She makes a tactical retreat into her shell as Milton leaps up onto the composing table and nudges Gutenberg's ink-stained hand. The printer grunts in surprise, having expected the cat to flee. He returns the broom to its place and strokes Milton.

"Just come for attention, have you? But I've no time today, my furry fellow. We're about to print my first book."

"We've only come to admire," promises Milton. "And they do say that black cats are lucky."

"Humph!" Gutenberg might protest but that doesn't stop him picking Milton up and settling him in his arms. Fortunately for Harriet and Milton, it turns out that Gutenberg is a cat lover. "And who's the other one with you?"

"That's Harriet, a tortoise."

One of the apprentices picks her up, getting inky fingerprints on her pristine shell. "She's clad like a knight!" he exclaims, tapping on her back.

"Oy! If you don't mind! Where I come from that's considered rude," says Harriet from within her shell.

"Well, if you are only here to admire, come with me and I'll show you my press," says Gutenberg, beckoning for the apprentice to carry Harriet into the backroom. She emerges to give the young worker one of her looks. Milton knows what that is like to be on the receiving end.

"Sorry," says the apprentice sheepishly. He places her carefully on a table with a good view of the new machine.

"I made the machine out of an old olive press – see that big wooden screw over there? That's to press the paper down firmly – and why we call it a press."

"Logical," purrs Milton.

"After we have set a whole page of the book in metal type, we place it on the bed of the machine and ink it over with my special formula ink," says Gutenberg proudly. The printer puts Milton down next to Harriet and picks up an inking stick. He flourishes it like a wand and a spot falls on Harriet's shell.

"This took me a while to discover. All the other inks either didn't stick well on the paper or smudged. I found that a combination of soot and turpentine mixed with walnut oil does the trick."

"And does it come off?" Harriet asks worriedly.

"Oh no," says Gutenberg. "It will last a very long time. These books should last for centuries."

"What! My shell is ruined!"

"Harriet, consider it a badge of honour," hisses Milton, not wanting to upset the printer while he is being so generous with his time on this historic day.

The apprentice who had knocked on her shell quickly wipes off the spot with a rag before it dries. "There you go. Only the slightest mark left behind. And it will fade after many washings." He holds up his grey fingers as proof.

"But I can't reach it!" moans Harriet.

Milton licks at the mark and wrinkles his nose. "That's not a nice taste. The things I do for my friends."

"Are we ready, boys?" roars Gutenberg, clapping his hands and spraying yet more ink around the shop.

His apprentices cluster around the machine, not worried that they are getting splattered. This is the moment they have all been waiting for.

"Then let's see if it works."

Milton now understands what the thumping noise he heard was: the apprentices testing the machine. With a thud, the machine presses down on the paper.

"We can make hundreds of impressions each day – maybe thousands when we get skilled at this. But first, the moment of truth!" Gutenberg lifts up the machine. "Little cat, would you care to make this a lucky day for us all by taking the first sheet off the press?"

Milton is bursting with pride. Gently, with the nimblest of paws, he removes the sheet of paper. Gutenberg takes it from him and lays it on a table to check the quality.

"What is the book?" asks Milton in a hushed tone.

"A Latin book to teach grammar," says Gutenberg. "I'm hoping, though, to do the Bible. That is the summit of any printer's ambition."

"Sensible to start with something modest," agrees Harriet, "so you can iron out the wrinkles in the process."

Gutenberg scans the page. "Boys: I think we're in business! It's perfect. Let's break for dinner. Beer and sausages are on me!"

It is late by the time Harriet and Milton arrive back at the time machine. The door opens only reluctantly and a message is waiting for them on the screen.

"I think the machine is jealous we didn't take it along," says Harriet, patting the console.

Milton is stuffed with sausages and has hiccups. "Or is it making a... *hic*... joke? You know, it's a... *hic*... time machine so all time is relative?"

The machine beeps and squawks indignantly.

"OK, I get the message. You were worried. Sorry." Milton curls up in a corner. "Wake me when we get to Italy. I might have some room for ice cream by then."

"Don't worry, Milton, you'll have plenty of time to digest," says Harriet. "We are going to make a brief stop in Frombork Castle in Poland first."

"What science gets done in a castle?"

"You'll be surprised. We are going to call in on Mikolaj Kopernik, known to most in the Latin form of his name: Nicolaus Copernicus. And I can promise you his ideas are earth-moving!"

It is late on a sunny day in 1510 when they arrive in the little town of Frombork on the north coast of Poland. The red brick walls of the castle and cathedral make a startling contrast to the green lawns. Long shadows stretch across quiet courtyards.

"Look out for a canon," says Harriet, stepping out of the time machine.

Milton ducks. "Don't tell me they are at war?"

"Not cannon. Canon!"

"You've lost me."

"One 'n' – job in a cathedral; double 'n' – weapon that can destroy cathedrals. Milton, you need a dictionary."

"No, I don't: I have you."

Harriet tuts but Milton can tell she is pleased with the compliment about her spelling ability.

The two friends hurry across the open spaces, not wanting to attract attention as explanations for their presence might take a very long time. Finally they track down the right canon on top of the castle battlements. He is waiting for night to fall and the stars to come out. As they watch, he adjusts his instruments.

"Why isn't he using a telescope?" whispers Milton.

"Those aren't used yet. The technology isn't up to the job."

"How can he make sense of the heavens with those instruments? What do they do?"

"Let's ask." Harriet clears her throat. "Excuse me, sir, what are those called?"

"Good evening." Copernicus looks around for the speaker, then finally looks down. "My, my, what extraordinary creatures you are!" Copernicus looks more carefully. "And you talk!"

"Consider us a dream," says Harriet quickly, not wanting to get caught up in explaining time travel to someone who is so influential on science.

"A waking vision," adds Milton.

"Inspiration for your great work," concludes Harriet.

"I suppose I have been working hard recently, trying to reconcile Ptolemaic Astronomy with what I see in the sky. But then, so many great thinkers have struggled." He sighs and puts his hands on his hips. "I suppose it is too much to expect a humble cleric like myself to come up with a solution."

"Oh no, sir. I'm sure you have as good a chance as anyone," Harriet reassures him.

"In fact, if I were a betting cat, I'd put my money on you," says Milton.

"Thank you for your encouragement." Copernicus tickles Milton under the chin. "Well then, visionary creatures, in answer to your question, I'm using a quadrant, a triquetrum, and an armillary sphere. I use the quadrant to measure angles up to 90°. The triquetrum helps me measure the altitudes of heavenly bodies. The armillary sphere is a model of the objects we can see in the sky.

"See here on the sphere? There's the earth, right in the centre." Copernicus scratches his head, looking between his notebook and the model. "The only problem is, my calculations and this model don't agree so I'm trying to work out what might make the two move in harmony."

Milton is bursting to blurt out the answer. Harriet steps on his paw to stop him.

"He gets there himself," she whispers. "Don't mess up the timeline."

"I'm about to produce a book outlining my calculations," Copernicus continues, "which suggests that one practical way forward for astronomers is to assume that the earth goes round the sun. It's an outrageous idea, obviously, but it solves a lot of mathematical problems."

"Sounds promising," says Harriet carefully.

"It is hard, though, to go against the brilliant work of the greatest of all astronomers, Ptolemy, to whom I owe so much, not to mention Aristotle whose model of the heavens we all learn at school. And there are many in the church who won't like the idea of such a radical change. With so many new books coming off the presses, the Pope is worried that the church will lose control of ideas. You have to tread very carefully."

"I'm sure you do," says Harriet.

"Others have come unstuck by going against the authority of the day," agrees Milton, thinking of the Greek scientists. "It's a good idea to be cautious."

Copernicus rubs his hands. "Excellent. My visionary creatures have confirmed my own instinct. I think I will leave my idea of a heliocentric, or sun-centred, universe as a theory and let the evidence of others' calculations prove or disprove the matter. That way I won't find myself at odds with my superiors."

Leaving Copernicus to make his evening's calculations, Harriet and Milton head back to where they left the time machine.

"So what do you think of his decision not to make a head-on challenge to the wisdom of the day that puts the earth in the centre?" Milton asks Harriet. "Is he being cowardly?"

"I think he is being sensible. He has the opinion that it is too much for one person to claim they have the answer. He wants support from other astronomers so he puts his theory out in a book for them to check. That's good scientific practice."

"What I find interesting is that his big picture of the universe is changing but he doesn't have complete faith in it being right. Part of him is afraid to challenge, not just the people in power, but also the great minds of the past, like Ptolemy and Aristotle."

"But there is a big change coming in Europe which makes people happy to do that. After that change, it became more natural to challenge Aristotle and other great thinkers with your own opinion."

"What change was that?"

"It begins with a priest called Martin Luther. He nails a list of 97 questions to a door in Wittenberg, Germany in 1517. That is the starting pistol for what is called the Reformation."

Milton thinks that sounds a daft thing to do – not to mention potentially criminal. "You can't just go round banging nails in church doors. Why did he do that?"

"In his day, it's like posting a news item online to invite comments. The church door is a public place so everyone will see. He has been led by his own study of theology to question some church practices. In short, he is claiming that, in his big picture of the world, the individual conscience trumps that of the Pope and the church."

"I can see how that might not be very popular with the people in power." Milton jumps up onto the castle wall and enjoys prowling along the top. He makes Harriet feel quite queasy as she is used to being low to the ground. "If ordinary people start thinking for themselves, reading books like the Bible on their own and in their own language, where will it end up? Shock, horror: we might even all get the vote!"

"Milton, you don't have the vote. You're a cat."

"Still, I can see a day when clever cats like me get the vote." He strikes a noble pose next to a coat of arms held up by a lion.

"Before that day comes, Luther's daring sets off two processes. First, there is new energy in the idea of thinking for yourself, and that helps scientists. The second is fear on the part of some people that change will overturn society and these freethinkers just need to shut up."

Milton jumps down and follows her into the time machine. "How rude!"

Harriet starts to enter the next destination into the machine. "And pointless because, if the truth is on the side of the person with a new idea, everyone adopts it eventually and the ones trying to stop it just look foolish. The Catholic Church does go on to ban Copernicus' books after his death, but happily for Nicolaus, he is left alone because he adopts his cautious approach of keeping it all theoretical."

"I'm glad to hear it. I wouldn't like to think that he suffers."

The time machine begins its familiar whirring as it sets off. Harriet sits back. "And they are far too late. Copernicus' works are already circulating so banning them is shutting the stable door after the horse has bolted. Protestant scientists from the new Luther movement are able to read them and even Roman Catholic ones get to know about them because scholars often ignore religious boundaries and keep exchanging knowledge and ideas."

"I bet the printing press also helps."

"That's right. Far more people can afford books thanks to the new technology and that means knowledge spreads. Let's go and visit one of these Lutherans and the next big name in our curious quest. Johannes Kepler."

As Milton and Harriet head to see Kepler, we are going to call in on Tycho Brahe, Kepler's employer and inspiration. He is a Danish nobleman who makes the astronomical calculations that prove crucial for the next big step forward in astronomy.

MEET THE SCIENTIST

TYCHO BRAHE

- Lived: 1546-1601 AD
- Number of jobs: 3 (astronomer, astrologer, alchemist)
- Influence (out of 100): 40 – spent 30 years making observations; he provided vital data for Johannes Kepler
- Right? (out of 20): 10 – calculations good but came up with a wrong model of the universe with Moon orbiting Earth, planets orbiting Sun but still with the sun going round the earth
- Helpfully wrong? (out of 10): 10 – great example of how good data still helps even if applied to wrong model!
- Interesting fact: famous for his false brass nose (he lost part of his real one in a duel)

Harriet and Milton arrive in the Austrian city of Linz in 1619. Snow is falling steadily and they hurry to get under cover.

"Remind me who we've come to see," prompts Milton.

"Johannes Kepler. He's a Lutheran teacher with a specialist subject in astronomy. Unfortunately, he has fallen out with some of the leaders in his church so spends most of the time employed by Catholic rulers."

"He thinks that it is his duty to search for the truth in the book of nature. Like Luther, he shares the big picture that you have to think for yourself even if it goes against tradition."

They enter Kepler's house and find him busy writing his Christmas newsletter for his family and friends.

As it is in German, Milton has translated it for me below.

Harriet

MILTON'S TRANSLATION OF "NEWS FROM THE KEPLERS"

Hello everyone. This has been a year of huge ups and downs. First the downs. I haven't been very popular in the Lutheran church because they think I'm very outspoken.

But worse

Mum has been charged with witchcraft! I know – outrageous! It's just that old

Ursula Reingold, from next door, is up to her old tricks. It looks seriously bad for dear old Mum. I'll have to swing to her defence.

Now on to the good news. I think I might have cracked the secret of planetary motion!

Thanks to my old master, Tycho Brahe, I've had excellent data with which to work and I found an 8-minute error in Mars' orbit. Disaster? No! It started me thinking. I now believe that Copernicus was wrong about circular orbits. Planets move in ellipses, speeding up and slowing down as they go round the sun. There must be one single simple magnetic bodily force making them do this, but what that is, I don't know.[2]

Friends, you can keep the kids busy after Christmas dinner with my little diagram of my three laws of planetary motion. They are in brief:

The orbit of a planet is an ellipse and the sun is at the centre at one of the two focal points. If you draw a line from the sun to the planet in orbit and measure the area

2 If you want to find out what this single bodily force is, look out for Isaac Newton in book 4 of *The Curious Science Quest*!

of a segment swept out over a given period of time, say a month, the area of that segment will be the same even though the distance travelled might be different.

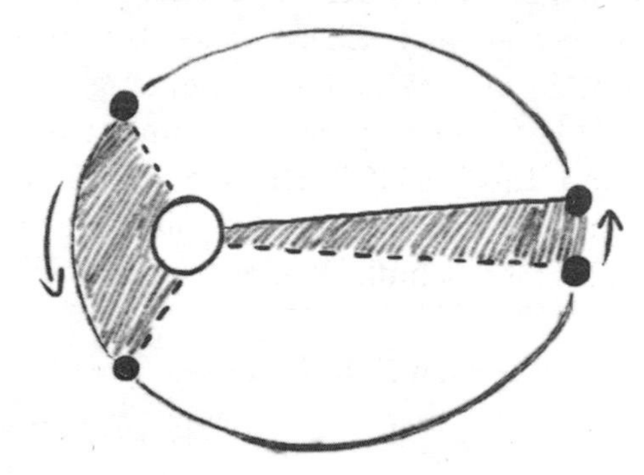

The third law is a little complicated for a Christmas letter but means that the relationship between the distance from the sun and the time it takes a planet to orbit round it is exactly the same for every planet in the solar system.

Pretty impressive, hey? But, as you all know, I'm not the pastor's favourite person ☹

so I'm going to do the calculations to show the future positions of the planets and let my theory become accepted because it is useful to astrologers and others interested in the stars. I think I'll call them the Rudolphine Tables.

Merry Christmas

Love Johannes

"Is that anything to do with Rudolph the red-nosed reindeer,? asks Milton hopefully when he's finished translating.

"Sadly not. Kepler named them after the Holy Roman Emperor, Rudolf II, who died shortly before publication."

Milton is feeling very Christmassy, thanks to the falling snow. The houses of Linz look like they might be made out of gingerbread. "Maybe the emperor was named after the reindeer?"

"Milton, stop. This has NOTHING to do with REINDEER!"

Milton folds his paws. "Ah, but can you prove that?"

Harriet walks off in a huff. "You're just being silly."

Harriet is frowning when Milton catches up with her in the time machine. He worries that he has teased her too much about Rudolph.

"Sorry, Harriet, I didn't mean to upset you."

The tortoise looks up, surprised. "Oh, Milton, I've been travelling with you long enough to know when you are just having fun. I'm not upset; I'm just wondering whether we should head to Italy now or make a brief stop in London."

"London doesn't have ice cream."

"No, but in 1605 it does have Bacon."

"I like bacon. And I liked Friar Bacon."

"This is another Bacon though: Francis Bacon. But London also has Shakespeare and I think a chance to meet him is worth putting off your dessert for a while."

"Me-ow! We get to meet Shakespeare! Even though this is a science quest?"

"It is a curiosity quest too. And Shakespeare was nothing if not curious. His plays reflect the questions of his day, and many of those are scientific ones." Her frown clears. "Yes, let's go to London. We will go to the premiere of *Macbeth* and meet Francis Bacon. Never say I don't show you a good time."

"Harriet, you show me the best!"

Shakespeare and Galileo: the Season Finale!

Harriet and Milton land on the south bank of the Thames and step out into the crowds hurrying into the Globe theatre. The circular thatched building is open to the skies with only the expensive seats under cover. The canopy over the stage is painted with the sun, moon, and signs of the zodiac. Milton doesn't think they look very scientific.

"Are we going to stand with the groundlings?" whispers Milton.

"We won't see much from down there but legs. I've a better idea. Our Francis Bacon is here, but as he is a nobleman he will be in one of the better seats. Oh, one more thing: as Kepler's mum shows, this age is worried about strange things that might be due to witchcraft. It is best if we don't go telling everyone that we are time travellers and that we can talk. You might be accused of being a witch's cat."

Milton mimes zipping up his mouth and nods.

They worm their way through the crowds of people standing and make their way to a seat halfway up the covered area. A man in a black doublet and hose sits on a bench. He is wearing a large white ruff. Milton nudges his boot and he looks down at them in surprise.

"Good gracious, has someone lost their pets?" The man picks Harriet off the floor so she doesn't get trodden on by the ladies and gentlemen crowding into the benched area. Milton jumps up beside him and purrs. "I can't return you just at the moment, little ones. We'll have to wait until the end of the performance."

The drums roll and the actors come on stage, three men

dressed as witches. From the very first word and throughout the three-hour performance, Francis and the two time travellers are riveted to the stage. Milton is so excited to be at the very first performance of this famous play that he barely remembers to keep the secret that he can talk. It has everything he likes: battles and ghosts, witches and villains, not to mention the wonderful words weaving the spell of the play.

The applause at the end is tremendous. Francis stands up and cheers. Milton dances from paw to paw. A bald-headed actor in the middle of the stage is given a special round of applause.

"That's Shakespeare!" squeaks Milton. "I can't believe I've actually seen him."

"Did you say something, little cat?" exclaims Francis.

Milton shakes his head vigorously.

Francis passes a hand over his brow. "I must have been working too hard to get my book ready for the press. I need a rest."

Waiting for the crowds to disperse, Francis sits back down. "Now that was a very interesting play." He strokes Milton absent-mindedly, happy to talk to the creatures he does not realize are listening. "*Macbeth* could be a warning not to read so much meaning into signs and wonders as it can lead ambitious people to evil. As I argue in my book, natural objects, like a tree or a bird, are here for their usefulness, not for their allegorical meaning."

"What's an allegorical meaning?" Milton whispers to Harriet.

"It means making an object into a picture or story to illustrate something else. Medieval thinkers did this all the time. They thought God used allegory in nature to tell us about himself and also about our place in the world."

"Allegory is the old way of thinking," continues Francis. "We need to go beyond the pillars of Hercules, leave the classical world of the Mediterranean, and sail uncharted seas to the New World. We have to advance learning so we all read nature in the language God actually wrote it in. We should not do this by allegory but by experiment."

Milton kneads Francis' velvet doublet with his paws, hoping

he'll say more.

"And how do we do that, you wonder?" asks the scholar. "We take measurements and test them. If they are true we can then work out general laws, or axioms, that lead to universal laws. Of course, there is every possibility of making mistakes but, looking out for fingerposts, we can be pointed in the right direction."

"Sir Francis, did you enjoy the play?" A fellow nobleman comes up to Francis and engages him in conversation.

"Time for us to go," says Harriet.

The two friends slip away and sneak back into the time machine. Milton chases his tail, still very excited about his afternoon at the theatre.

"Thank you for that treat! I enjoyed that even more than the Greek play we saw in Athens."

"And what did you think of Francis?"

"He is very nice and his doublet smelt of cinnamon."

"He is also a very clever man and helps establish the idea that, if you are seeking scientific truths, you need to read nature not for its stories but what it can tell us about itself. You do that through testing it and experimenting on it. That's the direction in which science is now heading."

Science to die for: How freezing chicken did for Francis Bacon

"It obeys the right fingerposts?"

"Yes, though there are still quite a few road blocks to come. That's the season finale to our little adventure in the Renaissance: Galileo and his big argument with the Catholic Church."

"And that takes place in Italy?"

"Oh yes. Milton, you are getting your wish. It is finally ice cream time."

They arrive in Rome in 1611 to find a party in progress in a cardinal's garden. A telescope has been set up so guests can look at the moon.

"Oh look!" cries Milton, bounding across the grass to take a peek at the sky. "They are using telescopes."

Harriet is puffing by the time she catches up. "Yes... instrument makers... have been working on the idea... but Galileo turned his mind to improving the lens. That's why he's been called the inventor of the spyglass."

TRY THIS AT HOME: SPY ON THE MOON!

Have you ever looked closely at the surface of the moon? Doing this was what started Galileo on his path to being one of the world's most famous scientists. Here's how to follow in his footsteps. Check a calendar to find the date of the next full moon (a couple of days either side will work too). Ideally, borrow some binoculars or a telescope but you can use your eyes too. Now see if you can spot the features that gave Galileo the idea that the moon is not perfectly round: valleys, plains, and mountains. Sketch them and, if possible, repeat on the following nights. Do the features look any different?

How did Galileo work out what they were? He noticed that the shadows changed – lengthened or shortened depending on how the sun's light was striking the surface of the moon. That told him that these objects had height and that meant the moon wasn't a perfectly smooth sphere as he'd been taught.

Galileo also teaches us to be careful when doing experiments. Not knowing the sun could permanently damage his eyes, he also turned his telescope in its direction. He discovered sun spots but also that it was a BAD idea to look that way. NEVER look directly at the sun, even if you are a scientific genius.

Milton has found a dish of ice cream on a side table. He leaps up and begins licking it before a waiter can chase him away.

"Hmm, lemon – delicious!"

Harriet is busy enjoying the summer evening – the music, the fireflies over the pond, and the treats served to the visitors. They pass in groups of colourful clerical robes, all heading towards the guest of honour.

"Hey! Get off of there!" A waiter shoos Milton away from the dessert table with a cloth. Milton jumps down and takes refuge with Harriet by an orange tree in a big pot.

"I hope the ice cream was worth it?" she asks, nibbling modestly on a dandelion leaf.

Milton licks his paws. "Oh yes." He looks around and takes in the guests clustering around Galileo. "Wait a moment – this party is being thrown by a church leader?"

"That's right. In 1611 the church doesn't feel threatened by Galileo's discoveries. In fact, they invite him to Rome and throw this big party. The relationship between science and the church is a roller coaster, sometimes up, sometimes down. Now you've had the ice cream I promised, let's go and hear what he has to say."

They find Galileo standing in the middle of a group of admirers. He is pointing up at the moon.

"If you use my telescope, you will be able to see for yourself that the heavenly bodies are not perfect or unchanging as Aristotle thought. They look like they are made from the same elements as Earth. I've even seen moons orbiting Jupiter."

"Are you saying there are no perfect heavenly spheres revolving in harmony? You dare to question Aristotle?" asks one young priest, looking a little pale at the suggestion.

"Indeed, I have to. I have tested his idea of falling objects and found them to be wrong."

"How, sir?"

"I stood at the top of the Leaning Tower of Pisa and tested the theory. I observed that objects of different weights fall at the same speed if dropped from a tower. Aristotle said the heavier would

fall faster. If Aristotle can be wrong about that, he can be wrong about other things too."

"We saw that somewhere before, didn't we?" whispers Milton.

Harriet nods. "Yes, John Philoponus did that experiment in Alexandria a thousand years ago. We almost got squashed, remember?"

"Hard to forget!"

"John's works are now translated and are available to scientists. It's highly likely Galileo has read them. But it's Galileo's statement of the proof that really takes hold in science so he is often credited as the first to show this. Ssh, he's got more to say."

"We, my friends, have to change our view of our place in the universe in light of these discoveries. You don't have to take my word for it; you merely need to look for yourself." Galileo's speech is applauded and a line forms to peek through the spyglass.

One churchman on the edge of the crowd doesn't look so happy. "But, Master Galileo, isn't what you just said contrary to what we read in the Bible?"

Galileo shakes his head. "I believe God gives us his word to teach us how to *go* to heaven, your eminence, and not how heaven *goes*."

"But... but that's not what we've always been taught - and taught to others," splutters the churchman.

"I'm afraid we'll have to change. We can't make things other than they are. Look through the telescope, your eminence."

"No thank you! I'm having nothing to do with this heretical nonsense!"

Galileo sighs. "If only he would read the signs God has given us. The book of the universe is written in mathematics for us all to read. Men like him shouldn't use scripture to frighten away the opponents of Aristotelian physics."

Harriet nudges Milton as the churchman stomps out of the garden. "That, I'm afraid, is a sign of what is to come for poor Galileo. Let's get back into the time machine and return in 1633. Galileo thinks that, because an old friend is now Pope Urban VIII, he will be able to persuade his opponents that the new model of the universe should be accepted. He has been told not to teach Copernicus but he thinks he can get around the restrictions by presenting his arguments in a dialogue."

"What's so special about a dialogue?" asks Milton.

"He can put all the different views without seeming to back one of them. The problem is, he didn't do a very good job! His preference is all too clear. Let's go and see him under house arrest waiting for his trial."

They find Galileo alone in his room, pacing in front of the window. It is a cloudy night.

"Excuse me, sir, I know it is a bad moment," says Harriet respectfully.

"Good gracious: a talking tortoise. I really must be dreaming!" Galileo rubs his eyes.

"I think that's as good an explanation as any," agrees Milton.

"And a cat! But if I say I hear cats talk, I'll be charged with witchcraft on top of everything else."

"Think of us as a waking dream," says Harriet soothingly. "You look like you need to talk to some friends."

"I do indeed. Things aren't going at all well for me."

"Can you tell us why you are in trouble?"

"It's this book." He gestures to the one on his desk. "The Inquisition are going to ask me questions about it at dawn. I don't have much time to change their minds."

"What's it called?" asks Milton.

"*A Dialogue Concerning the Two Chief World Systems*. The two are Aristotle's model versus Copernicus': the old one with Earth at the centre or the new where the planets orbit the sun."

"What's in it?"

Galileo settles back to tell his side of the story. "I thought I was being very clever. You see there are three friends talking: Sagredo, who is neutral, Salviati, who is most like me in his views, and Simplicio. I named him after the famous scholar from Alexandria who defended Aristotle."

"Oh yes, I remember him," says Harriet with a scowl.

"I started off on the first day with my telescope finds. They liked those a few decades ago. On the second, the characters discuss the objections to the idea that the earth moves. On the third, they see how Copernicus' model gives a better account for planetary motion. On the fourth, they discuss tides."

"So what got you into trouble with your old friend Urban?" presses Harriet.

"Pope Urban has his own views on the subject of the heavens. Some say he became upset that I put his ideas in the mouth of Simplicio. He thought I was making fun of him."

"And were you?"

Galileo strokes Milton. "I've never been known for my tact. Others say, though, that Urban is under pressure to show he is a strong leader who can clamp down on dissenters. Being my friend means he has to be doubly firm with me." Galileo sighs. "But do you know the most frustrating thing? I know I am right! I thought I could leave the arguments to speak for themselves. I've done a thousand experiments and demonstrated it a thousand times."

"Sometimes politics get in the way of the truth," says Harriet.

"Are you telling me that it won't go well at my trial?" asks

Galileo. There is a knock at the door. "There's my guard now, giving me my five-minute warning that they are coming to collect me. What should I do? Tell the truth or agree to endorse a lie because I am afraid of the consequences?"

He isn't really talking to them, Milton realizes. "We'd better go," he says.

"Yes, sadly we can't change the outcome," agrees Harriet.

Leaving Galileo to contemplate his cloudy skies, Harriet and Milton get back into the time machine.

"What happens at the trial exactly?" asks Milton.

"The ones scared of changing the big picture win. Galileo is put under house arrest, ordered to reject his views, and forbidden from publishing any more books."

"That's a very big uh-oh moment!"

"One of the biggest, and the church's reputation struggled to recover. Despite setting up universities and encouraging many scientists over the centuries, it is moments like this for which the Renaissance Church is remembered."

Milton licks his paws thoughtfully. "But was the dispute really about science?"

"Excellent question! These moments never are simple. The Catholic Church had long been a great supporter of astronomy, and Galileo remained a devout Catholic to the end of his life. We mustn't make the mistake of caricaturing it as a conflict between science (Team Galileo) and religion (Team Pope). Those were not separate categories then and the people involved wouldn't recognize our picture.

"What was really happening was that Copernicus' views were gaining supporters across Europe, with people like Kepler using the mathematical model for practical purposes. Galileo had the misfortune to misjudge the way he presented his evidence. He was going too fast for his audience, and being too optimistic that proof would win over people to *his* big picture when they were used to seeing the world another way."

Milton folds up the timeline Harriet had given him and tucks it away in his drawer of keepsakes. "I'm confused."

"About what?"

"That can't be the last word. Today everyone knows that the earth goes round the sun. How did something that was a massive problem for Galileo become generally accepted and completely uncontroversial?"

Harriet smiles. "I'm glad you asked that. To find the answer, we will need to head back to England."

"Will there be good snacks?"

"I can promise at least one apple. That's because we are going hunting for the secrets of the universe with Newton."

Where to go to find out more

There are lots of helpful websites that will tell you more about the people, objects, and places mentioned in Milton and Harriet's quest. Here are a few to start you on your own curiosity quest:

National Geographic for Kids. This comes as a magazine but also has a website with lots of fun articles, quizzes and competitions: **https://www.natgeokids.com/uk/category/discover/science/**

Another fun site goes behind how things work. It has some sections that would appeal to a medieval mind, like the article about "If unicorns were real, What would they use their horns for?" **https://science.howstuffworks.com**

Or if you want to take a curious free app with you on your phone, have a look at the collection put together by The Exploritorium in San Francisco: **https://www.exploratorium.edu/explore/apps**

The Science Museum in London also has a collection: **https://www.sciencemuseum.org.uk/games-and-apps**

Gutenberg may have started the first printing press in Europe, now we have the Internet to spread our news! You can keep up with scientific news at this website: **https://www.sciencenewsforstudents.org**

If you'd like to try more experiments at home, this website is clearly presented and has some great ideas: **http://www.teacherstryscience.org/kids**

For older readers
If you'd like to read about the history of science in more depth, you might like to try: *The Penultimate Curiosity, Roger Wagner and Andrew Briggs* (OUP, 2016)

Answers
How many times did you spot the Curiosity Bug? The answer is 15.

Meet the authors

Julia Golding is a multi-award-winning children's novelist, including the *Cat Royal* series and the *Companions Quartet*. Having given up on science at sixteen, she became interested again when she realized just how inspiring science can be. It really does tell the best stories! This is her first experiment with non-fiction but hopefully her collaborators, Roger and Andrew, will prevent any laboratory accidents.

Andrew Briggs is the professor of nanomaterials at the University of Oxford. Nanomaterials just means small stuff. In his laboratory he studies problems like how electricity flows through a single molecule (you can't get stuff much smaller than a single molecule). He is also curious about big questions. He flies aeroplanes, but he has never been in a time travel machine like the one that Harriet and Milton use – yet!

Roger Wagner is an artist who paints power stations and angels (among other things) and has work in collections around the world. He didn't do the drawings for these books, but like Milton and Harriet he wanted to find out how the 'big picture' thinking of artists was connected to what scientists do. When he met Andrew Briggs the two of them set out on a journey to answer that question. Their journey (which they described in a book called *The Penultimate Curiosity*), was almost (but not quite) as exciting as Milton and Harriet's.

Harriet and Milton continue
their quest in

HUNT WITH NEWTON